Bee-bim Bop!

by Linda Sue Park
Illustrated by Ho Baek Lee

Houghton Mifflin Harcourt
Boston   New York

Library of Congress Cataloging-in-Publication Data

Park, Linda Sue.
Bee-bim bop! / by Linda Sue Park ; illustrated by Ho Baek Lee.
p.   cm.
Summary: A child, eager for a favorite meal, helps with the shopping.
ISBN 0-618-26511-2
[1. Cookery, Korean — Fiction. 2. Koreans — Fiction. 3. Stories in rhyme.] I. Lee, Ho Baek, ill. II. Title.
PZ8.3.P1637Be 2004
[E] — dc22   2003027697

HC ISBN-13: 978-0-618-26511-4
PA ISBN-13: 978-0-547-07671-3

Printed in China
SCP 30 29 28 27
4500824024

To Jackson and Margaret
—L.S.P.

For everyone who loves Korean food
—H.B.L.

Almost time for supper
Rushing to the store
Mama buys the groceries—
more, Mama, more!

Hurry, Mama, hurry
Gotta shop shop shop!
Hungry hungry hungry
for some BEE-BIM BOP!

5

Home and in the kitchen
Eggs to stir and fry
Mama, catch the spatula—
flip the eggs high!

6

Hurry, Mama, hurry
Gotta flip flip flop!

Hungry hungry hungry
for some BEE-BIM BOP!

9

Rice is on the boil
Bubbling in the pot
White and sticky-lickety
Steaming good and hot!

Hurry, flurry rice
Gotta pop pop pop!

Hungry hungry hungry
for some BEE-BIM BOP!

11

12

Mama's knife is shiny
Slicing fast and neat
Garlic and green onions
Skinny strips of meat.

13

Hurry, Mama, hurry
Gotta chop chop chop!
Hungry—very hungry
for some BEE-BIM BOP!

15

Spinach, sprouts, and carrots
Each goes in a pan
Let *me* pour the water in—
yes, I know I can!

17

Sorry, Mama, sorry
Gotta mop mop mop
Hungry—in a hurry
for some BEE-BIM BOP!

Bowls go on the table
  Big ones striped in blue
    I help set the glasses out
      Spoons and chopsticks too.

20

Hurry, family, hurry
Gotta hop hop hop!
Dinner's on the table
and it's BEE-BIM BOP!

22

Quiet for a moment
Papa says the grace
Everybody says "Amen"
A smile on every face.

Rice goes in the middle

Egg goes right on top

MIX IT!

MIX LIKE CRAZY!

Time for

BEE-
BIM
BOP!

BEE-BIM BOP (rice topped with vegetables and meat)

There are as many versions of bee-bim bop as there are families who cook it. This recipe is one that we make at home. Please don't let the number of steps scare you—none of them are difficult.

Mung bean sprouts, sesame seeds, *ko-chee-chang*, and *kimchee* are available at many large supermarkets as well as at Asian grocery stores.

INGREDIENTS (serves 4)

2 cups white rice

Marinade
    2 cloves garlic, peeled
    2 green onions (scallions)
    5 tablespoons soy sauce
    2 tablespoons sugar
    2 tablespoons vegetable oil
    1 teaspoon sesame seeds, roasted (*optional*)
    1 tablespoon sesame oil (*optional*)
    1/8 teaspoon black pepper

Meat
1 pound tender, lean beef (such as sirloin tip)

Vegetables
    2 carrots
    2 pkgs. frozen spinach, defrosted,
      or 1 pound fresh spinach, washed
    1 pound mung bean sprouts

Other ingredients
    4 eggs
    salt and pepper
    vegetable oil for frying

Serve with
    ko-chee-chang (Korean hot-pepper paste, *optional*)
    kimchee (Korean pickled cabbage, *optional*)

COOKING INSTRUCTIONS

These instructions are for you and a grownup to follow together.
Cutting up ingredients and using the stove should be done only by the grownup.

1. **You:** Pour 2 cups of rice into a rice cooker or a pot. Add 4 cups of water. If you have a rice cooker, put the lid on and press the button.
   Grownup: If you are using a pot, put the pot over a high flame until the water boils, then lower the flame, cover the pot, and let simmer for 20–30 minutes until the rice is tender and all the water has been absorbed.

2. **Grownup:** Mince the garlic and chop the green onions.
   You: Mix all the marinade ingredients in a big bowl.

3. **Grownup:** Slice the beef across the grain into very, VERY thin slices.
   You: Put all the beef into the bowl with the marinade. Stir well with a big spoon. Wash your hands. Then stick your hands into the bowl, grab handfuls of beef, and squish all of it around for 2–3 minutes. This makes it nice and tender. When you finish, wash the marinade off your hands. Set the beef aside.

4. **You:** Break the eggs into a large measuring cup. Throw away the shells. Beat the eggs with a fork until the whites and yolks are completely mixed together.

5. **You:** Put 1 teaspoon of vegetable oil into a small nonstick frying pan.
   Grownup: Put the pan over a medium flame. Let it heat for about 1 minute. Pour about 1/4 of the egg into the pan. Rotate the pan quickly so the egg spreads out in a thin layer on the bottom. Cook the egg for 1 minute. Using a wide spatula, flip the egg over and cook the other side for 1 minute. You now have an egg "pancake." Flip the pancake out onto a cutting board and leave it there to cool. Repeat until you have used up all the egg, adding a little more oil if needed. You should be able to make at least 4 pancakes. Leave them on the cutting board until cool enough to handle.

6. **You:** Put the egg pancakes on top of each other to make a neat stack. Roll up the stack tightly.
   Grownup: Cut the roll into 1/4-inch slices.
   You: Put the slices into a medium-sized bowl, unroll them, and toss them around a little. They will look like a bunch of yellow ribbons. Set aside.

7. **Grownup:** Using a vegetable peeler, peel the carrots. Then cut them into julienne strips (small sticks about 2 inches long) with a knife or in a food processor. Heat 1 tablespoon of vegetable oil in a large frying pan or wok over a high flame and stir-fry the carrots over high heat until tender. Empty the carrots into a bowl and set aside.

8. **You:** If you are using frozen spinach, squeeze some of the water out of it.
   Grownup: If you are using fresh spinach, cook it for 2 minutes in a pot of boiling water, drain, and let cool for a few minutes, then squeeze some of the water out. Put 1 tablespoon of vegetable oil into the frying pan and stir-fry the thawed or precooked spinach for 2-3 minutes until tender. Empty the spinach into a bowl, season it with salt and pepper, and set it aside.

9. **You:** Pour one cup of water into a large saucepan. Add 1/4 teaspoon salt.
   Grownup: Put the pan over high heat. When the water boils, put the bean sprouts into the pan. Cover the pan and cook for 2-3 minutes. Drain the bean sprouts and empty them into a bowl.

10. **Grownup:** Put the large frying pan over high heat. Heat the pan for about 30 seconds. Take the bowl of beef and marinade and dump it into the frying pan—all of it at once. When the beef hits the pan, it will sizzle loudly. Using a spatula or a wooden spoon, spread the beef out in the pan. Stir for 2-3 minutes until all the red meat turns brown. Turn off the heat. There will be cooked beef and some gravy (meat juices) in the pan.

To Serve

Put the rice, the bowls of egg strips and vegetables, and the pan of meat where everyone can reach them. Each person puts a pile of rice in the middle of a soup bowl or plate and some meat and vegetables on top. (Be sure to pour a couple of spoonfuls of meat juice on your rice.) Top with egg ribbons. If you like spicy food, add some *ko-chee-chang* (hot-pepper paste).

Now "bee-bim"—mix everything together. It's ready to eat (with some *kimchee* on the side, if you wish)!

AUTHOR'S NOTE

Bee-bim bop is a popular Korean dish. *Bop* is the Korean word for rice, and *bee-bim* means "mixed up." So "bee-bim bop" means "mixed-up rice." It's a favorite meal for many Koreans.

Each diner gets a portion of rice, then tops it with meat, steamed or stir-fried carrots, green vegetables like spinach and mung-bean sprouts, eggs that have been made into flat omelettes and then shredded, and *kimchee* (pickled cabbage). When all the food is on the plate, you *bee-bim*—toss and mix everything together like crazy—to make a colorful and delicious meal.

The author with her nephew and niece, Jackson and Margaret Hubble.